Rosie the Raven

Helga Bansch

Rosie the Raven

translated by Shelley Tanaka

annick press
toronto + berkeley + vancouver

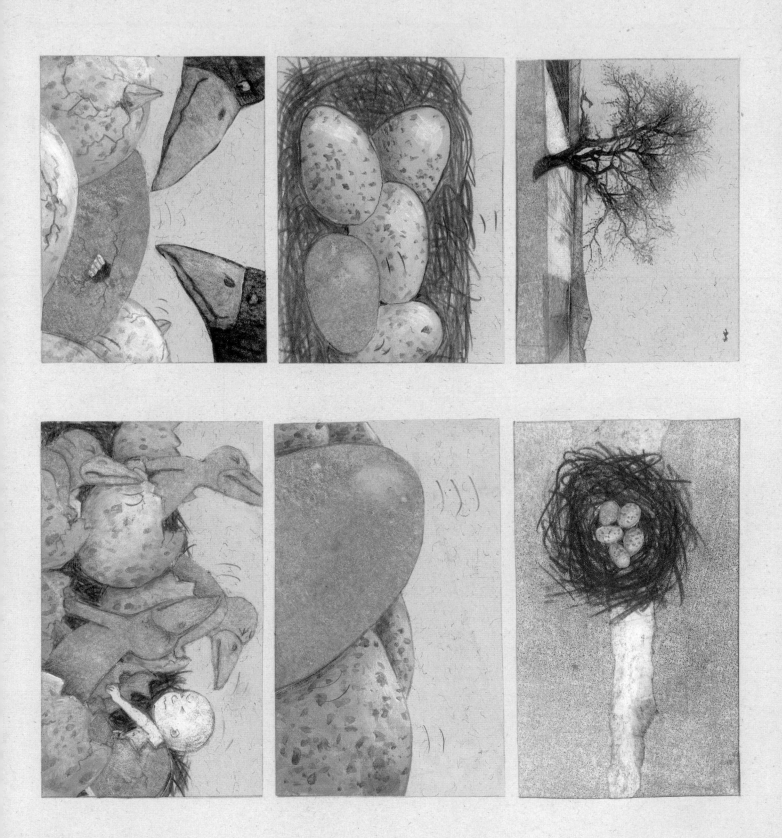

Our nest was high up in a tree. As soon as we hatched out of our eggs, Mama and Papa took us under their wings. It was nice and warm there.

My brothers and sisters opened their beaks wide. I was hungry, too, so I did the same. We ate worms, flies, maggots and snails.

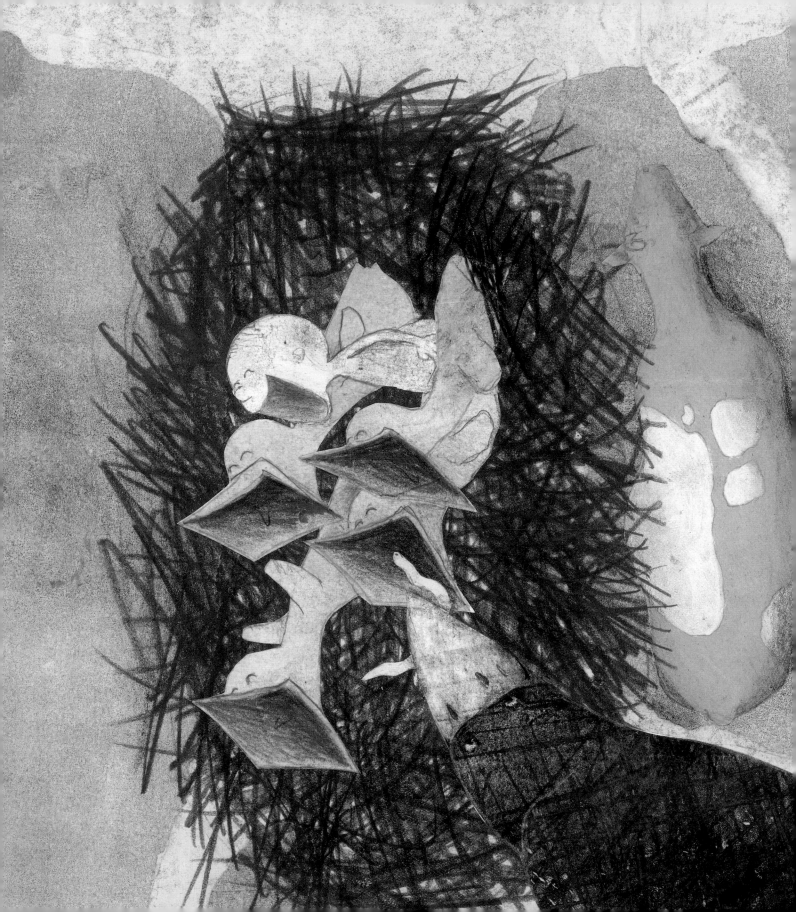

The rest of the time we slept, had cawing contests and goofed around. I was always cold, so Papa got me a dress and a hat.

"Our little Rosie," Mama called me.

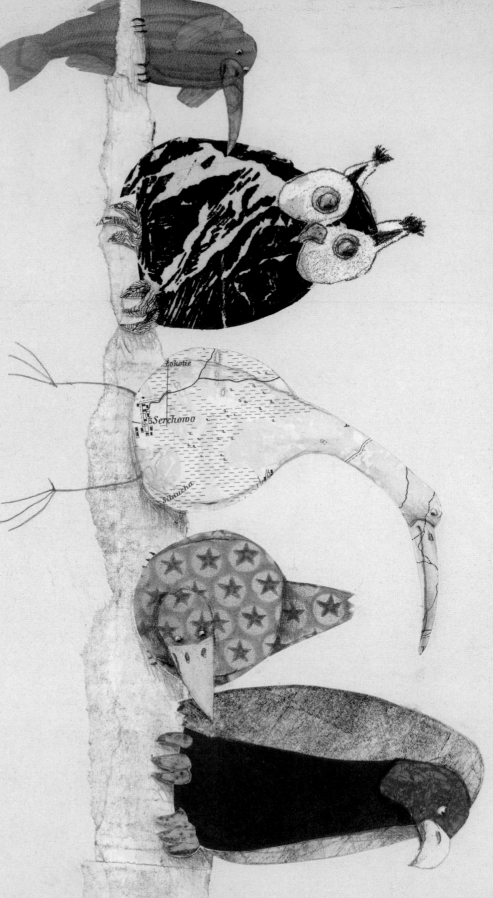

Every day others would come and stare at us.

"Poor little worm," they whispered. "It needs to exercise its wings." Or, "It's pretty ugly. Rub it with birch leaves. That will make its feathers grow!"

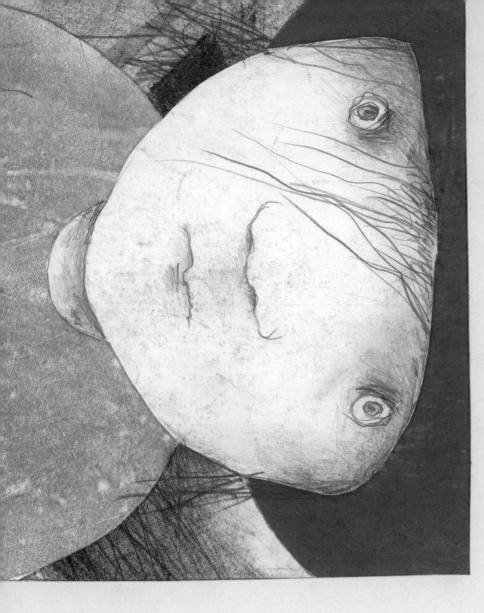

At first I had no idea what they were talking about. So I looked at myself, and then I looked at my brothers and sisters. And for the first time I noticed I was different.

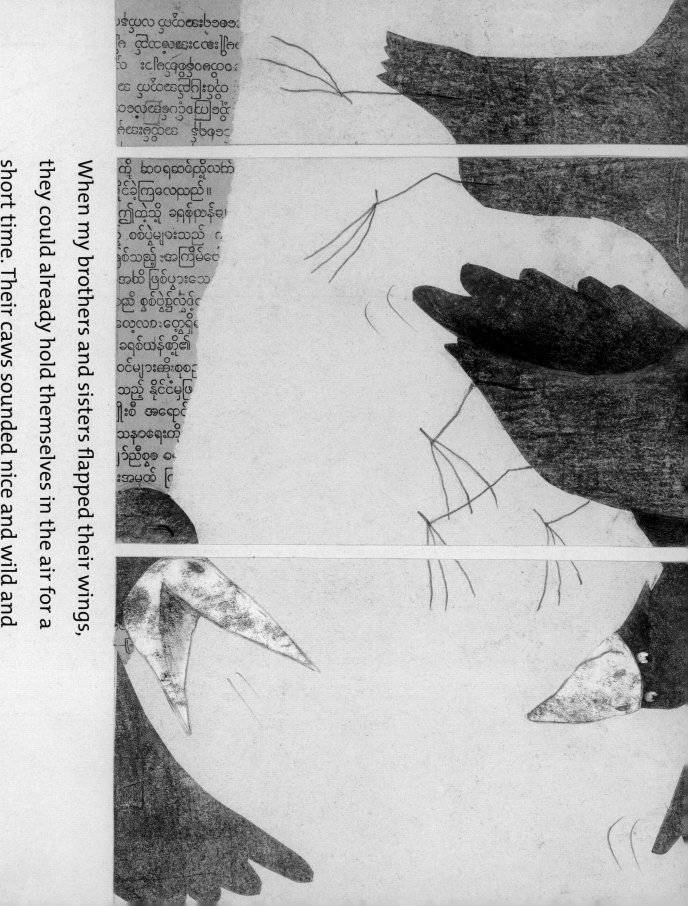

When my brothers and sisters flapped their wings, they could already hold themselves in the air for a short time. Their caws sounded nice and wild and harsh, and their feathers were fluffy and soft.

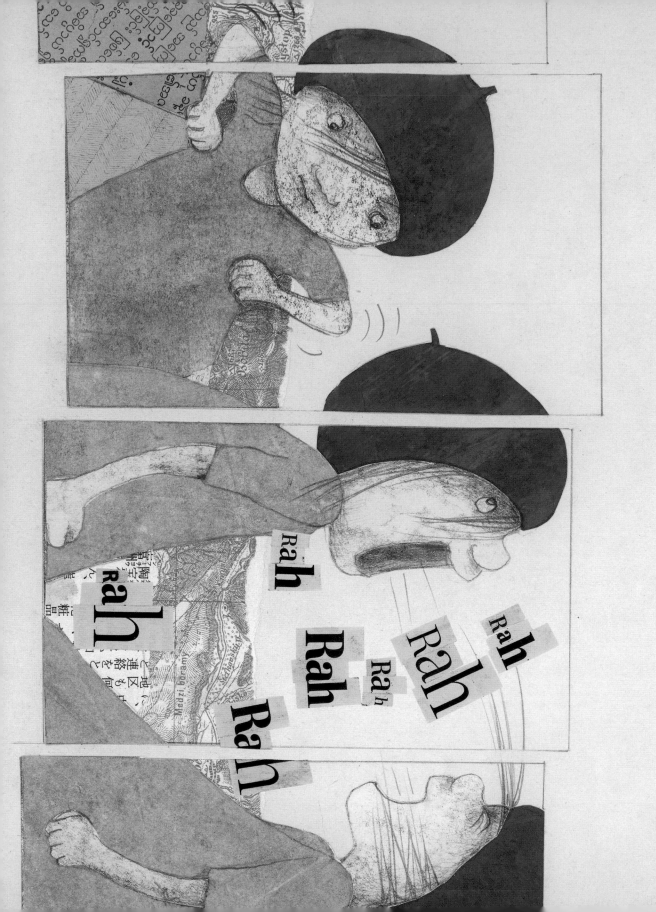

When I flapped, nothing happened. My voice sounded pitiful, and I had no fluff. No feathers!

I so wanted to be like them. I tried to beat my wings, over and over. I cawed until I was hoarse. I rubbed myself with birch leaves until my skin was as green as grass for days.

But soon I decided all this was just silly.

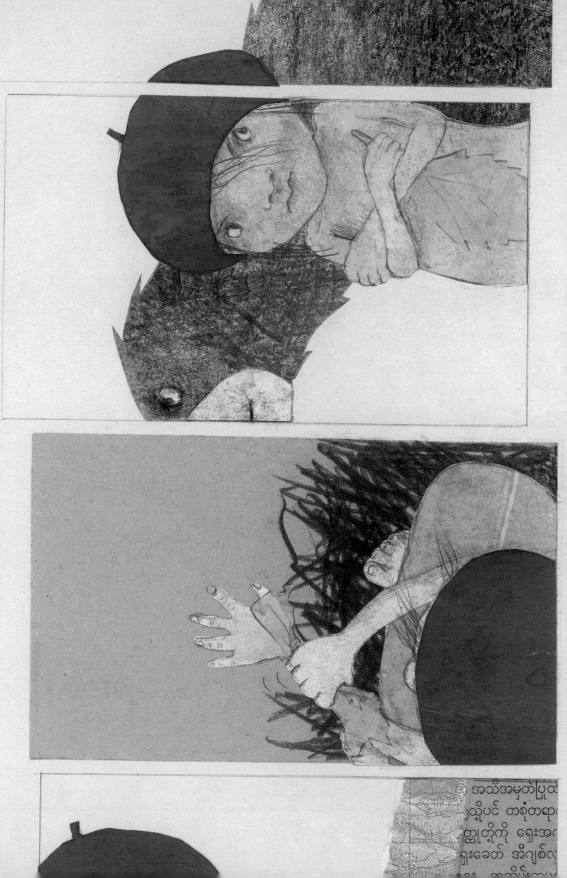

"Yeah, so?" I thought. "I'm just different.

And if the others talk about me, what do

I care?"

Besides, I found out that my kind of

wings were quite useful for other things.

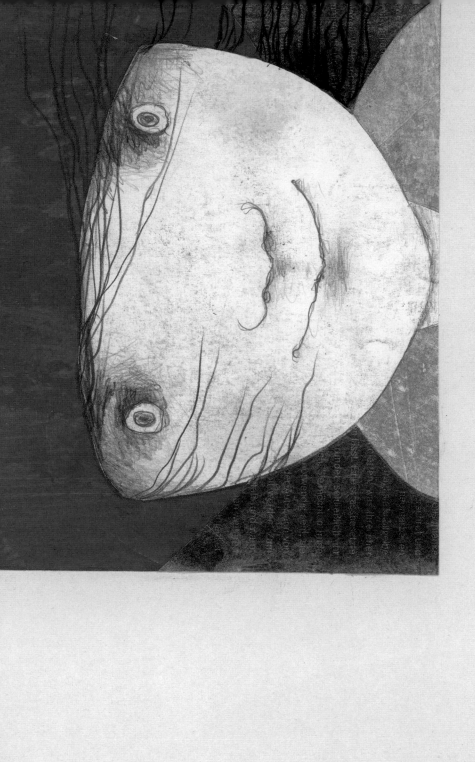

A few weeks later, my brothers and sisters took off into the world. It was very quiet in the nest without them.

When the air began to smell like autumn, it was
time to set out for the south. My parents practiced
staying in the air with me on their backs. I nearly
fell to the ground, and that gave me a scare!

But gradually it started to work.

Finally they said, "When the sun comes up, we'll be off!"

I was so excited, I didn't sleep a wink.

The next day our trip began. We soared high over snow-covered mountains, dark forests and green meadows, and on to a big sparkling sea. First class all the way!

Our new home is in a tree that's perfect for climbing. I'm the one who collects the food now. We're going to really need it soon, because the new babies are about to hatch. There are four eggs in the nest.

Today I met a frog by the lake. Tomorrow he is going to teach me how to swim.

When I turned to go home, he called after me: "So, what are you, really?"

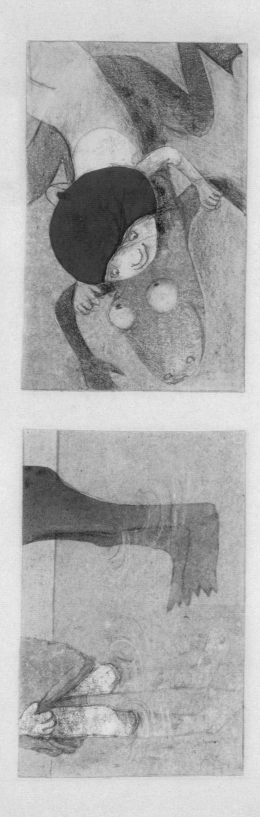

"I am Rosie the Raven!" I squawked, nice and loud.

Then I went home and climbed up to our nest.

I can't wait until tomorrow!

© 2016 Verlag Jungbrunnen Wien

Title of the original Austrian edition: *Die Rabenrosa*
English translation © 2016 Shelley Tanaka

The art for this book is a collage of pencil drawing, acrylic paint, monotype, and old maps.

Cataloging in Publication

Bansch, Helga [Rabenrosa. English]   Rosie the raven / Helga Bansch.

Translation of: Die rabenrosa.
Issued in print and electronic formats.
ISBN 978-1-55451-834-0 (bound).—ISBN 978-1-55451-833-3 (paperback).—
ISBN 978-1-55451-835-7 (html).—ISBN 978-1-55451-836-4 (pdf)

I. Title. II. Title: Rabenrosa. English.

PZ7.B234Ro 2016   j833'.92   C2015-904837-0
                                        C2015-904838-9

Distributed in Canada by University of Toronto Press.

Published in the U.S.A. by Annick Press (U.S.) Ltd.
Distributed in the U.S.A. by Publishers Group West.

Printed in China

Visit us at: www.annickpress.com

Also available in e-book format.
Please visit www.annickpress.com/ebooks.html for more details.
Or scan